First published 2011 by Walker Books Ltd
87 Vauxhall Walk, London SE11 5HJ

2 4 6 8 10 9 7 5 3 1

© 2011 Brun Limited

The right of Anthony Browne to be identified as author/illustrator of this work has been
asserted by him in accordance with the Copyright, Designs and Patents Act 1988

This book has been typeset in Gill Sans

Printed in China

British Library Cataloguing in Publication Data:
a catalogue record for this book is available from the British Library

ISBN 978-1-4063-3017-5

www.walker.co.uk

How Do YOU Feel?

Anthony Browne

WALKER BOOKS
AND SUBSIDIARIES
LONDON • BOSTON • SYDNEY • AUCKLAND

How do you feel?

Well, sometimes I feel **bored** …

and sometimes I feel

lonely.

Sometimes I feel very happy ...

and sometimes I feel *sad*.

I feel ANGRY ...

and sometimes I feel **guilty**.

Sometimes I feel curious …

THE MOST
DANGEROUS
POP-
EVER!!

but then sometimes I'm **SURPRISED!**

I feel **CONFIDENT** ...

but I can also feel *shy*.

I can feel a bit worried ...

but more often I feel REALLY **SILLY!**

Sometimes I feel very hungry …

and sometimes very **FULL**.

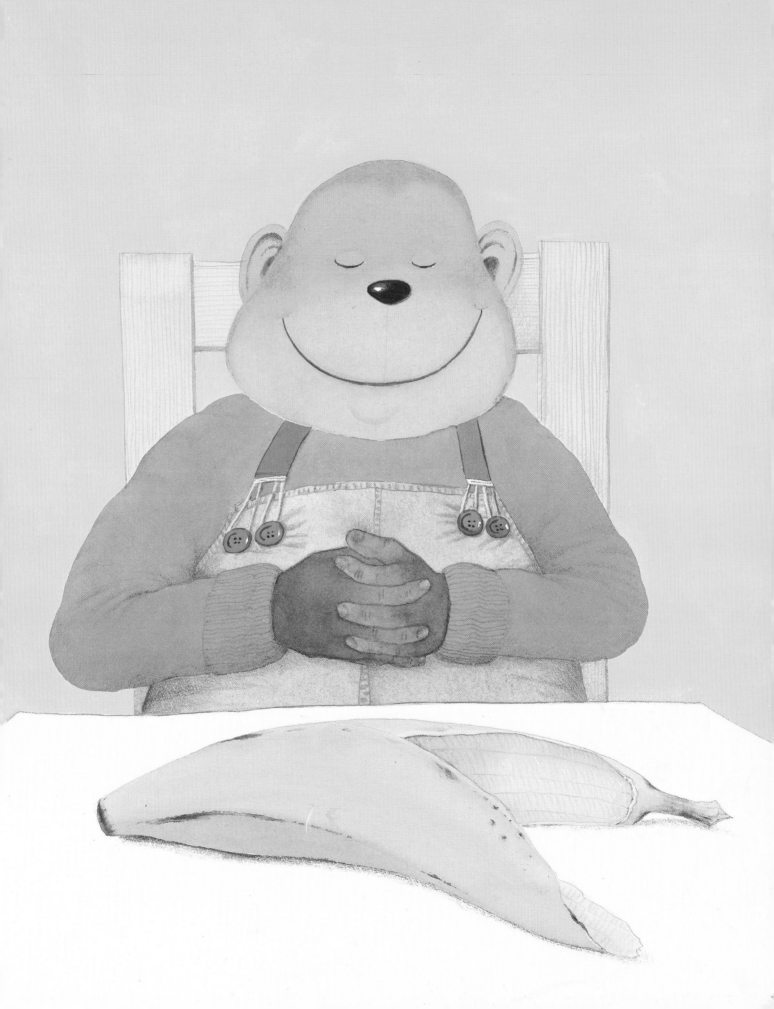

Right now, I feel a little sleepy.

How do
YOU
feel?

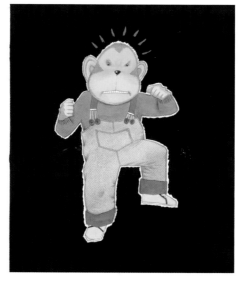